GRAVE TIDINGS

SALEM SINCLAIR

I LOVE YOU

♥ Salem Sinclair

Cover Design: Claire Holt at Luminescence Covers
Editor: Amy Briggs, Briggs Consulting LLC
Formatting: AJ Wolf Graphics

To all the people like me that looked at Krampus and asked, "Aye, what that tongue do?"

TRIGGER WARNINGS

Uhh, monster goat cock? Improper use of Christmas lights and tinsel.

Hanging ornaments from questionable places. Misuse of mistletoe.

Umbrella warning applies for kink and BDSM but know that nothing too heavy or negative happens.

Playlist

Candles in the Snow — Nox Arcana

Jingle Bells (Dark Piano Version) — Myuu

Santa Claus Is Coming to Town (Dark Piano Version) — Myuu

One Dark Christmas — Mark Russell

Poisoned Mistletoe — Mark Russell

Starlight Waltz — Derek Fletcher

Echoes of Elise — Nox Arcana

Krampus is Here — Myuu

Sleep Tight — Chris White

Snowman (Slowed, Remix) — Lofis

The Krampus comes forth, ringing thine bell
From out of the darkness, resounding from Hell
Displaying thy rictus, switchel in hand
A demonic vision now walks the land.
Unknown

CHAPTER ONE

It was the night before Christmas in Grimlake and the only creature stirring in the snow-covered town, Noelle was sure, was her.

And this *Krampus-forsaken* tree.

Noelle huffed as she repositioned her hands on the trunk of the evergreen and gave a heave, dragging the tree further up the concrete steps that led to her newly rented townhouse.

She wouldn't even be in this mess if her fucking boyfriend of three years hadn't suddenly ended things and kicked her out like a stray dog a week before the holiday.

"Fuck these steps, fuck this tree, fuck Craig, *fuck Christmas*," Noelle gritted out. Why she suddenly decided to add a bit of holiday cheer to her home at the last minute, she could not remember, but she had heavy regrets.

The idea had seemed so simple — buy a tree, set up the tree, enjoy the twinkling lights as she drowned her sorrows in spiked eggnog. What she hadn't accounted for — and in hindsight, she really should have considered — was that it *was* Christmas Eve and most tree farms were already closed. Finally, after an hour of searching she located a small, shady-looking tree stand set up at a gas station that had one sad, mangled tree left. The burly guy manning it had assisted her in lifting the tree atop her car and tying it down tightly. What she hadn't considered was how difficult it would be to remove the tree from the roof of her vehicle plus drag it up the numerous steps leading to her brownstone building.

At this point, Noelle was contemplating just dropping the tree and letting it slide back down the icy stairs because the mere idea of dragging it through the front door and attempting to set it up on the tree stand exhausted and enraged her.

But goddammit, she was not a quitter.

Energy renewed by spite, Noelle rolled her shoulders and cracked her neck. Grasping more tightly onto the lower branches on the trunk of the tree, she grunted as she reared back with all her strength…

Only for her foot to catch a piece of ice and slip out from under her.

With a startled yelp, Noelle went down hard — ass

to concrete, feet over head — and groaned out pitifully as a throb started up instantly in her lower back. To her horror, she heard the cracking of branches and shush of pine needles against stone as the tree slid down the flight of stairs once more.

"*Fuck you!*" Noelle hollered to the glittering stars in the sky and to Santa Claus, wherever he was out there, for ever going along with this stupid holiday. She tossed up two middle fingers to the big jolly guy in case he didn't get the message the first time.

"My, what a blunt offer," came a gravelly yet jovial voice from somewhere below Noelle's sneakered feet.

Noelle's back twinged as she sat up suddenly to identify the speaker.

A man, swaddled up tightly in a form-fitting grey peacoat stood in front of the fallen Christmas tree, hands in pockets as he surveyed the wreckage of Noelle's night with gleaming eyes.

The twinkling lights strung from lamppost to lamppost glistened on the freshly fallen snow that littered the dark strands of his hair. His jaw was sharp and shadowed with stubble. His skin was a warm brown, with golden undertones so rich Noelle knew it was natural versus brought on by time spent in the sun. She couldn't quite make out the color of his eyes from the distance, but some odd trick of the luminescent snow mixed with the lights caused them to reflect strangely.

"Uh, I—no. I'm sorry," Noelle stumbled on her words as she painstakingly climbed to her feet, keeping a close eye on the icy patches. She clutched tightly to the exterior brick of her building and looked down at the man again. His shiny black shoes were inches away from the damaged tree as he inspected it and Noelle in turn.

"I wasn't cursing at you, just—" she waved an arm around to encompass the tree and their surroundings.

A finely groomed brow arched high. "Everyone else in the world?"

Despite her bad mood, Noelle felt a smile tug at her lips. "Basically, yes. It's been...a day..." She trailed off with a heavy breath.

"Not feeling the merry spirit of the season, I take it," the stranger remarked. His voice was gravelly and rolling, with an accent Noelle couldn't place. Something European, she mused.

"I think if Santa were giving out an award for the least jolly person in the world, I would likely win it today," Noelle admitted. "Call me Ms. Scrooge. Better yet why not name me Krampus's mistress. I am all jollied out."

A deep hum rumbled, seemingly coming from the man's chest, something so akin to a purr that Noelle started. But the man said nothing further and gave no hint the noise came from him, so she figured what she'd heard must've come from a rumbling engine.

I need some eggnog and some sleep, she thought.

Then Noelle groaned out loud as she remembered *the fucking tree*. She couldn't just leave it down there at the base of the steps, half blocking the sidewalk… Could she? Maybe she could. Or, maybe she technically *shouldn't*, but she could…

As she mused the technicalities of whether leaving a Christmas tree on city property was littering, the man's voice reached her ears once more.

"Would you like some help?" he offered, extending a hand toward the bane of her existence.

Hope lit her chest for a moment. "Oh my god, really? Please. That would be — oh my god, seriously, so much help. You have no idea how long it took me just to get it up these steps. And then I dropped it again." Noelle released an exasperated breath, breath puffing out and blowing the red fringe of her bangs back from her face.

"Honestly, I was about to give up and just leave it there," she acknowledged, smiling at the man when he chuckled.

"The situation did appear dire when I came upon you playing turtle and cursing at the sky," the stranger mocked.

Noelle gasped. "Playing *turtle*?" Then she pictured herself in her mind; how she must have looked, flat on her back, arms up and middle fingers pointed high at the blanketing of stars. A laugh burst out of her.

"You were quite convincing. For a moment, I truly thought you immobilized on your backside." He bent down and without even a grunt, hefted the tree over his shoulder and started up the steps, maneuvering carefully to avoid slick spots. Bells jingled as he walked and Noelle spotted what she assumed was a keyring hanging out of a pocket. The dangling bells jangled against his thigh with each step.

Mouth hanging open, Noelle watched in stunned silence as the apparent Hulk in disguise casually carried the evergreen up to her landing. That peacoat must be hiding some serious muscles, she speculated.

At the man's polite cough, Noelle jumped, realizing she had been staring in awe and not moving to open the front door so they could enter.

"Oh! Yeah, sorry. Let me just —" she dug her keys out of her coat pocket, mittened fingers sliding silkily over the metal key as she rushed to push it into the knob.

Once it clicked over and the knob turned under her hand, she flung the door open and stepped back.

"Is it okay if I just —" the man motioned toward the foyer of her townhome with his head as both hands were clasped tightly around the tree.

"Yes! Please, please go on inside. I'll follow you and

close the door."

Noelle watched as pine needles rained down on the hardwood floors as he walked through the door frame and the fir's branches were squeezed tightly together.

Once the tip of the evergreen was through the door, she stepped inside and shut the door behind them while instructing him to turn left into the living room. Prior to going out on her tree hunting expedition, she had gotten all the decorations out of her storage unit and dropped them off so multiple red utility tubs lined her living room walls. The tree stand sat in the corner, next to the raw edged wooden mantle that hung over the electric fireplace slotted into the wall.

Apparently, Noelle had left it on when she'd made her hasty decision to run out this evening because the fake flames were still flickering, casting shadows across the room. Heat pumped out of the electrostatic lungs, warming the chill the icy winter wind had left behind from the door being open.

As the pair made their way into the living room, Noelle cleared a path through the strewn décor for the man until he could settle the trunk firmly in the base of the tree stand.

"I'll hold it here if you'll tighten the screws," her helper said. So, Noelle dropped down and, crawling on her hands and knees, arched low until her upper body was beneath the skirt of the lower limbs. She could feel them tickling her back even through her coat. One branch caught the edge of her jacket as she wiggled deeper beneath the tree, hands outstretch as she blindly reached for the anchors, and dragged it up her back.

Noelle groaned internally, imagining what she looked like from behind.

Here was this unbearably attractive man helping her with her tree while she was face down, wide ass up, in ratty leggings with her love handles sticking out over the band for everyone to see.

Please don't let these be the leggings with the hole in the crotch, she prayed as her fingers finally latched onto the hooks and she began twisting them tightly.

"Is it getting tighter?" Noelle asked, grunting as she kept turning the anchors until they locked into the trunk.

"So tight," came the growling reply from above her. "But I think it could be tighter. Let me adjust my grip so the tree goes in...deeper."

The sound of movement came from above her and then she felt a nudging at her ankles. At the prodding, she automatically spread her legs without thinking twice. Before she had realized what she'd done, the man's foot stepped between her thighs, so close the leather toe of his shoe nearly touched her crotch. She jerked her hips further up to avoid sitting on his foot, only for her center to rub against his shin.

Noelle gasped at the sensation.

It was unexpected and yet still sent a jolt of pleasure arcing through her.

She tried to move away again only for the leg to press against her more tightly.

"This is the perfect position," said the stranger. His voice was rough, so deep now that Noelle felt the bass vibrations echo in her bones. "Tighten the screws for me."

As the tree slid deeper into position, so did Noelle's hips as her arms reached out further. Up her hips titled until her clit was nearly plastered against the man's leg. He didn't move an inch, keeping the tight pressure right there.

Noelle wasn't naïve by any means. This man had to know what he was doing…right? Had to know what the maddening pressure against her center would be doing to her as her body wiggled slightly with the movements of her arm.

When she realized that her whole body moved with the tightening motions, she exaggerated them, rubbing herself more firmly against the hard shin and trying to make it appear accidental. She kept huffing in tiny, short breaths, hoping that her panting would go unnoticed until…

Until what?

Was she just going to rub one out on this guy's leg?

Without him *knowing*?

Gross, Noelle. Shame on you. Shame on your family. Shame on your cow —

Sighing, Noelle twirled the last anchor once more until it would turn no further and then began attempting to back her way out from under the tree.

"Don't stop," the man growled.

"The screws are tightened. It should be done," she replied, uncertain.

"That's not what I meant."

Heat flooded her as she immediately grasped his unsaid words. He knew exactly what Noelle had been doing up against his leg and he wanted her to continue?

Torn, Noelle debated.

On one hand — it had been months since anything besides good ol' B.O.B had buzzed her to an orgasm, way before she and Craig broke up.

On the other — this man was a stranger. She didn't even know his name. Luckily for her and her aching clit, that could be easily remedied.

"What's your name?"

"You can call me Gus." His voice was still cave deep. The rumbling tone made her bite her lip and throw caution to the wind.

If *Gus* was okay with this, then she was too.

So, Noelle stretched out further, sliding her knees wider and letting her hips open deep so her pelvis could drop down until her cloth-covered clit touched that polished, shiny dress shoe. Bracing herself on her elbows, she began rocking her hips.

Slowly, at first.

Building up the pleasure.

Back and forth, back and forth her slit ground against his foot. She felt herself dampening, the short glide across the toe of his shoe growing slick as cream lined her underwear. Panting breaths broke free from her mouth along with small mewls of pleasure. Noelle tried to keep the noises in, mortified enough already by her wanton actions.

But Gus didn't let that slide. His voice seemed loud after the silence. "Let me hear you."

"What?" Noelle gasped.

"Take your pleasure freely, but do not withhold anything. I want to hear your sweet cries." His toe lifted with a sudden, hard pressure that made Noelle cry out. "Just like that. Be a good girl and make that sound for me again."

And Noelle did.

As her hips rotated, seeking only her pleasure, noises poured from her lips with abandon. No longer did embarrassment stall her from pursuing the pinnacle she sought. With her body angled as it was under the tree, she was unable to lift herself up and sit down fully on his foot; to get the intense contact she craved.

She widened her stance further, pushing her hips to the limit of their flexibility as she dropped the front of her body to the ground, so she was laying nearly flat, breasts pushing brutally hard into the wooden floors, and pelvis angled up so that the button at the apex of her thighs dragged just right over his shoe.

"That's it," Gus purred. "Rub your cunt against my foot. So horny you can't help but rut up on me like an animal."

Shame burned through her at his words, at being compared to a mindless, rutting beast, but her hips didn't stop moving. She was too close now.

Noelle's muscles were burning with use but she pushed through the pain, panting out pleas she wasn't even aware she was uttering. Begging Gus to fuck her, to end her torment, to help her finish. In an act of mercy, he began moving his foot in counter to her rotating hips.

"*Fuck*," she moaned. "Yes, yes, yes."

The heat from the fireplace and the coat she still wore was overwhelming her. She felt faint as she neared release. Sweat beaded at her temples and pooled in her lower back.

And *there*. God, she was so close. Noelle could feel the orgasm glittering at edge of her periphery, just a few more moments —

But suddenly Gus was pulling away, his foot and it's delectable, firm pressure leaving her shaking as the shining star of her climax hurtled further out of reach.

"No!" Noelle hollered. She reared out from under the tree, sweaty and red-faced, and pissed. "I was so close, please"

The man she'd invited into her house just gazed back at her haughtily. And that was when she noticed something she hadn't before. His eyes, previously hidden in the shadows of the night, were now fully visible and rather obviously very *not* human.

They burned the same red of a Yuletide fire but were slitted like a goat's.

"Oh, sweet Noelle. Naughty girls don't get their full pleasure until they take their punishment. And I've heard you've been a very naughty girl this year," the man crooned.

And she realized, all at once, who she had invited into her house.

Gus von Krampus. The twin shadow of Santa Claus.

CHAPTER TWO

When she first moved to Grimlake three years ago, Noelle did so knowing that monsters lived next door. This town was one of the few shared spaces of the world where supernatural beings and humans mingled and coexisted peacefully. She had initially moved here for Craig—who himself was a brownie—and stayed even after the breakup because Grimlake was beautiful.

Noelle had run into various creatures over the years, from werewolves to centaurs and even one angry unicorn that she'd startled when out on a run in the park, but she never suspected she would come across one of the big power players of the preternatural world.

And Gus von Krampus was certainly one of those. His name was whispered on the streets in fear and awe. While his brother, Nicholas, was the patron saint for all things good and happy, Krampus was the dark side of the coin, St. Nick's henchman when do-gooders did wrong.

The fact that he was here, in her house, meant she'd really displeased the jolly ol' guy.

"You know my name," Noelle whispered. The arousal had drained from her body and in its place was a fear so deep, so primal, it made her very bones tremble.

Krampus stared at her coolly; his red eyes menacing even as he backed away from the tree, slowly unbuttoning his coat. As he shook it off, she couldn't help but take in his wide shoulders and trim waist beneath the black, collared shirt he wore. No tie adorned his neck so the top three buttons were undone, giving Noelle a tantalizing glimpse of the golden skin gleaming in the firelight

With his teeth, he bit at the tip of his leather gloves and off they came, giving her the first glimpse at the set of lethal claws adorning his fingers.

"Darling, of course I know your name," Krampus admitted, his accented voice rumbling out from that deep chest as he unbuttoned a cuff and pocketed the golden cuff links in his trouser pocket.

With care, he began to meticulously roll up the sleeves of his shirt. Veins stood out starkly against his muscular forearms and for a reason Noelle refused to admit, she found it hard to swallow as she eyed the strength beneath that bronzed skin.

"What's that silly song you humans sing about a list?" He inquired but it appeared to be a rhetorical question as he carried on speaking without waiting for an answer. "The naughty or nice list, I believe? Not *quite* what my dear brother is concerned about, but he does certainly keep tabs on people and my, oh my, little lamb, you have irked him something fierce."

"Me? How!" Noelle blurted, fear set aside for a moment as outrage took over. "I've never even been in trouble at work, much less with the law. How did I end up on the naughty list?"

Krampus hummed as he contemplated. "Something about cursing him repeatedly? This is his big night, you know. He doesn't take kindly to foul words being spewed when he's working hard to make children happy across the world."

Dumfounded, her mouth gaped open. "Wha—no! I mean, *yes*, I said a couple of…of bad words, maybe, but I was just angry! I was having a really bad week." Tired of sitting down and feeling like she was being belittled like a child, Noelle stood.

What she wasn't expecting was the immediate locking up of her hips and knees as she straightened. Apparently, her ligaments and muscles had not yet recovered from their overuse from her earlier activities. Her body pitched forward, directly into the waiting arms of Krampus.

He clucked his tongue. "Poor little lamb. Having such a tough time of it."

Clutched against his chest as she was, she could feel the thudding of multiple hearts behind his rib cage. A black claw perched below her chin, tilting it up so she was looking directly into those eerie, animal eyes of his. As she watched, his stunningly handsome face began morphing.

Darkness crept onto his skin like an ink spill, stealing away the golden tone and leaving behind a color akin to coal. Horns grew from his head, huge and ram-like, twisting backward away from his face in a spiraling curl. White, brightly gleaming fangs grew in his mouth and a cruel smirk lit his face and Noelle wondered if he was admiring the fear in her face.

Gus von Krampus, even halfway into his beastly form, was a sight to behold.

Long, luxurious locks of moon-pale hair poured from his scalp, flowing around his horns. Braids of varying sizes dangled in the mass of tresses, interwoven with silver threads of tinsel and small bells. Krampus was a palette of stark colors—coal dark, snow white, fire red—and he was fiercely beautiful.

The intensity he exuded caused chills to erupt

across Noelle's body.

His claws stroked the tangly mess of strawberry-bright hair away from her face as he cooed at her, "Unfortunately, for you, your tough day is about to get even worse."

Body tensing, Noelle rapidly began shaking her head back forth as she pushed against his firm, warm chest, arching away from him.

"No, please," she started, but Krampus shushed her with a finger to her lips.

"Begging won't save you now, pet. You must take your punishment like a good little girl. Are you going to behave for it?"

Noelle knew she should concede, should give in, and behave. But fear was a powerful motivator and she didn't want to be punished; didn't feel like she did anything deserving of punishment. So, with a yell, Noelle head butted the creature before her and scuttled out of his grip.

She heard an angry mutter behind her as she raced from the room and down the hall, but she didn't take the chance to peek back and see if he had started after her yet. Yanking open the front door, she tore down the slick stairs, slipping and sliding, crashing onto the landing with a painful thud. Her leggings tore open at the knees as the concrete dug in. She paid it no mind, just scrambled to her feet, and took off at a sprint down the street, yelling for help.

"Help! Please, help me! It's the Krampus!" Noelle cried out, terror causing her voice to crack. Her heart was in her throat and in her ears, booming so loudly it nearly drowned out every other noise.

Suddenly: laughter. Deep, and rough, sounding from everywhere and nowhere. "Oh, pet. I do love a good chase. Run," the voice growled. "Run faster."

And she did.

Adrenaline warmed her blood as she veered from the suburban streets toward the icy forest. As Noelle stopped behind a tree to catch her breath, she glanced behind her, wincing at the track marks in the ankle-deep snow that led directly to her.

"You better watch out, you better not cry," said Krampus in a slow, eerie singsong tone.

Still unable to tell where he was at, Noelle focused on how to cover up her tracks instead of locating the shadow creature. She spied a downed balsam fir branch and moving swiftly, snatched it up and began walking backwards, dragging the branch along to cover her tracks in the snow.

"You better not pout, I'm telling you why…"

It wasn't a fool-proof guarantee, but Noelle hoped that this would give her enough coverage that her prints would be less discernible. When she came upon a large, snow-covered evergreen with a full skirt, she ducked under it, dropping the broken branch just as Krampus voice sounded right outside of the bough she hid in.

"Krampus is coming…" Thunderous hooves sounded right outside her hiding spot.

Clasping her hands over her mouth, Noelle tried to stifle her panicked breaths. The forest was silent beyond the frozen branches swaying in the wind and the deep, huffing breaths Krampus was releasing from his barrel of a chest. She could just make out pieces and parts of him between the pine needles and prayed that he couldn't hear the roar of her blood as it thundered into her heart.

Suddenly, between one blink and the next Krampus was gone. Unwilling to believe she had lucked out that easily, Noelle stayed hidden within the branches until her breath returned to normal and her pounding pulse turned steady.

Such time had passed that the previous adrenaline rush was waning, leaving her trembling and cold in the forest so she gathered her reserve of courage and stepped out beyond branches, looking this way and that.

Huge hoof prints were imprinted into the snow, the size of dinner plates at least, and she stared at them warily, but also with wonder. She knelt to trace the ginormous print.

"…to town." The words were whispered on the

back of her neck and Noelle let loose a bloodcurdling scream that was stifled by a palm clasped against her mouth. She tried to bite the palm, but her teeth had little to no effect against the thick skin.

"Ooh, little lamb. You've been extra naughty," Krampus purred against her temple. He held her tightly against him, back to chest, with one arm clutched around her waist and pinning her arms to her side and the other still covering her mouth. "Consider your measure for punishment extended."

Noelle whimpered against his palm as tears gathered in her eyes.

An unnaturally long, red tongue dipped out and swirled up her cheek, lapping at her tears.

"Save your tears, pet. You'll need them when you beg me for mercy."

And with a tap of his claw against her forehead, Noelle was out like a light before she could give his words any further thought.

CHAPTER THREE

When Noelle came to, it was all at once and with the understanding that she was cold. Within moments, she became aware of why.

Going by the breeze chilling her body, she was *nude*.

"What the fuck!" she cursed. Or would have, had something not been forcing her mouth open. It was wide and round and tasted of metal. Noelle grunted in fear, tongue lolling freely in her mouth around the cage holding it open. The more noises she made, the more drool she produced and as she couldn't swallow it properly, it just dripped down the sides of her mouth.

"Lamb, your squirming is so enticing. Wiggle your ass some more for me," Krampus said from behind her, voice like gravel. Then a clinking sound, almost as if he were setting a glass down.

Noelle tried to turn her head but couldn't—a sharp tug against her scalp prevented her from moving. As she panted in confusion, she paused to take stock of the situation. She strained her eyes to look around, trying to figure out where she was when she caught sight of a chair nearby. Understanding dawned — she was in her dining room.

She was on the *goddamn table*.

Moving each part of her body slowly, Noelle soon realized that she was trussed up like a Christmas turkey.

An ache had been building in her shoulders and she finally grasped the reason behind it — her arms were folded back behind her, tied seemingly at intervals with what felt like rope. She wiggled her fingers, pleased to know she still could, despite the tingly feeling in them. When she attempted to move her legs, her upper body swayed some and she realized suddenly that her bindings held her suspended above the table. Just a few inches, but high enough that her nipples barely grazed the shining wooden surface.

And her breasts, they felt full and heavy. When she arched her back as well as she could, she understood that there was something constricting each breast. Tied so tightly around them they felt like balloons about to pop. All the blood in her chest was rushing to her nipples and every maddening glance against the table caused Noelle to groan, despite herself.

Connected to the binds squeezing her breasts was a strap firmly tied around her shoulders, almost in the shape of a vest going by the rough friction against either side of her neck where the rope draped. This portion of her bindings appeared to be attached to the table legs to prevent her from swaying in the air freely.

Noelle's knees were spread wide, pelvis angled upward, and as she wiggled her hips, she noticed a tug around her waist that also jerked lightly at her arms. All the fastenings appeared to be connected somehow, so that when one part of her body moved, another part of her felt it.

The same pulsating rush of adrenaline that had overtaken her in the woods as she ran from Krampus zapped back into her veins like electricity and she whined around the item in her mouth as the feeling overtook her.

"Hush, pet. We're just getting started with your punishment," came Krampus's voice once more, just as a clawed hand reached and gripped the meaty part of her rear, where her thigh met her ass. Mortification washed over Noelle at the realization that in her current position, her pussy and ass were bare and on vulgar display for the creature. "What a beautiful present you make, all wrapped up like this."

That's when she clued into the fact that the soft, ethereal glow she could make out of the corner of her eyes were the Christmas lights he had woven around her.

"And this…" She felt a finger lightly tug at the hoop she had pierced through the hood of her clit. "Is especially enticing. Let's make this a little more… festive, shall we?"

Unsure what he meant, Noelle just panted harshly around the gag in her mouth, trying to catch a glimpse of him without any luck. She felt his fingers messing with the piercing and the contact, against her will, sent sparks of pleasure through her. Suddenly, she felt a weight tugging against the hoop and every tremble of her hips caused the heavier hoop to glance off her clit.

As Noelle was unable to turn her head to the side, she instead ducked down to look down her body, beyond her purpling, swollen breasts that were constricted with rope, to the bright red ornament she could see dangling between her thighs.

Krampus had used her piercing like a tree branch to hook the decorative item from.

A keening wail racketed from Noelle's chest, more from embarrassment than anything else. And the one thought that tumbled through her mind, above all else in this ridiculous situation, was that she wished she had shaved.

"Yes, yes. Tell me about it," the creature said conversationally, as if Noelle had spoken aloud instead of just whined piteously. "Your life is horrible, you don't know how you ended up in this situation, you're not this kind of person, et cetera, et cetera. I have only heard the same diatribe a thousand times over the years, so I wised up. Started gagging the naughty listers."

As he spoke, the sound of a chair scraping backward caught her ear and then those large hooves took slow, measured steps around the table. His hand trailed over her body the entire time, making goose flesh ripple across her skin, unbidden.

When he came to a stop before her, Noelle could just see the black fur of thickly muscled thighs standing before the table at the edge of her peripherals.

A single finger stroked down her cheek, then her chin, gathering up the drool that was freely running from her mouth. Another shock of utter shame sparked through her and this time, for some unknown reason, she felt it jolt directly in her cunt.

"Now then, pet. Let's discuss some rules of punishment and your safe words and cues. Oh, I know what you're thinking—"at this point his voice went into a high falsetto— "'A safe word Mr. Krampus? But I don't even want the punishment!' to which I reply: too bad, so sad. Can't do the time, don't do the crime, or however the saying goes."

"I may be here to mete out punishment, but even I have limits. Nothing I do will truly maim or permanently scar you, whether that be physically or mentally. When you feel as though you've reached your pain threshold, curl your right hand into a fist, with your first two fingers extended. The scene will stop immediately. If you're nearing the threshold but want me to slow down instead of stop, make the same gesture, but with only one finger extended." Krampus ran a hand over Noelle's head, petting her like a dog.

"Make the gestures. Show me you understand what I'm asking."

Fingers trembling, Noelle made each gesture without even pausing to consider why she obeyed immediately.

"Absolutely perfect. Good girl," he purred right into her ear. She trembled as his breath stirred the fine hairs near her lobe.

Then, with a cruel laugh, Krampus slapped her ass, leaving her spinning with the sudden brutality.

"Let's begin."

Apparently, Noelle mused, the beginning was not coming anytime soon.

After the slap that left her reeling, Krampus had tied a dark band of cloth around her eyes, blinding her. He seemed to disappear after that; she couldn't even hear him breathing.

Strung up and blind, Noelle's mind conjured all horrible manors in which Krampus was planning on punishing her and she found herself getting worked up. A new rush of fear slid through her veins, potent and overwhelming, as she fussed behind her gag. She knew it sounded like she was sobbing, and maybe she was.

She wasn't sure anymore.

Time passed, fast and slow all at once. All Noelle could focus on was the ache in her joints, the burning feel of the rope around her sensitive flesh, and the rapid pulse that echoed in her ears. Her breasts were throbbing, but more than that, she acknowledged, they ached to be touched. The barely-there graze of her nipples on the table was infuriating; she craved for a deeper rub, something to soothe the soreness.

Desperate for more sensation, Noelle jerked at her binds, crying out when there was no relief. To her utter mortification, her pussy clenched and unclenched, and she felt wetness ooze out of her. Her thighs were damp and cool in the open air, the slipperiness matching the drool falling, unheeded, from her mouth.

Noelle felt crazed, her mind buzzing with the lack of visual and auditory sensation even as her body was overcome with physical stimulation.

Was this his punishment? She wondered. *I don't know if I can take more of this.*

Pleading cries fell from her mouth. She prayed that Krampus was nearby and could hear the desperation in her tone. Noelle had wanted to do well, had wanted to accept whatever he doled out to show him she could handle it, but she fucking lied.

She was done.

She was going to call it quits.

She was going to use the cue he taught her to get out of this and be done.

But just as she started to fist her hand, there was a sudden *pop* along with a change in the air current, a clattering of hooves on the floor, and with a vicious slap, Krampus's hand came down right on Noelle's defenseless clit.

CHAPTER FOUR

Noelle screamed.

She screamed as the pain rushed from her throbbing, swollen clit with the piercing, through her overstimulated body and sent her hurtling into an unexpected, endless orgasm. It roared through her in massive waves, unlike anything she had ever experienced before.

When she climbed down from the peak, still trembling with aftershocks, it was to find Krampus's hand lovingly caressing her rump. Two fingers swiped down the center of her, gathering her juices, and she heard him groan before the sound of lip smacking filled her ears.

Was he...tasting her?

"You taste sweeter than the candies the elves whip up, little lamb. Devine." Krampus grabbed a handful of each generous ass cheek, spreading her wide as he spoke. His claws pinched as they dimpled her skin. "Mmm. I can't wait to sip on more of you."

Groaning low in her throat at the idea, Noelle arched her back, trying to press closer to him. The previous orgasm, while delicious, had not sated the need coursing through her body. All that pent up adrenaline, all that fear — it turned sharply into arousal and it was burning right through her core.

The need within Noelle was powerful, so heady, that she moaned again, slipping down the slope of surrender. She tried shaping words around the metal cage in her mouth, begging Krampus to touch her sopping wet pussy, but they only came out as inaudible, whining noises.

As he rubbed and groped her ass and thighs, he avoided the place she desperately wanted him to touch the most.

"Let's get you nice and warmed up, pet," Krampus cooed to her, slapping a hand down on her ass cheek lightly. "Fifteen spankings and then we'll try the switch, yes?"

Noelle adamantly shook her head no.

"Hmm, no switch? Are you sure? Good girls that accept each level of punishment get orgasms…" His voice trailed off as a clawed finger grazed over her clit, making her jump. "Does that sound like something you want? Want to come for me?"

She sobbed out her answer on a wail, pussy clenching around nothing as a fresh burst of wetness dripped down from her opening.

"Going to make you come so good on my tongue, little lamb. Remain obedient. Accept your punishment." As he ended his sentence, two hard swats landed on her rump, first one cheek, then the other in quick succession.

The suddenness caused her to cry out more so than the sharp sting his palm left behind. He rubbed a hand over the burning spot, once, twice, before *wham*! Another strike of his palm against tender flesh. After each impact, he would soothe the skin with a quick rub before spanking her again.

Finally, when she was a twitching mess, Krampus said, "Five more to go. Brace yourself."

But before she could, his hand struck with double the force it had previously. Noelle shrieked at the contact, her whole body jerking against her restraints. Another impact, and another, one right after the other with no pause, no release, no time to prepare.

These hurt differently than the previous spankings, deeper, almost. This was a bruising, aching pain and Noelle wondered if she would be able to sit down tomorrow. The stiffness in her joints was nothing compared to the rawness of her ass cheeks right now.

Two more teeth-rattling slaps from his massive

hand and then his towering frame was leaning over her prone form so he could whisper into her ear, "So good for me. Now it's time you earned a reward. But first—" He paused his words for a moment and she felt a sudden loosening in the tightness against her shoulders as she was being lowered down to the table like a dolly— "Let's get you untied and settled into a new position, hm?"

As her ballooned breasts touched the table, Noelle twitched, groaning at the pain in her shoulders as the rope loosened in increments. Finally, when all the bindings around her arms were removed, Krampus assisted Noelle in bringing her arms down to her side, massaging the feeling back into them with surprisingly gentle strokes.

Endorphins fogged her brain as blood rushed back into her muscles and her stiff joints moved as Krampus tenderly rotated both arms for her, checking their ability to move. He began working at the ties around her chest next, unrolling the numerous bands of rope from around each strangled breast. Once her breasts were freed, he reached out, wrapping the long length of her hair around his wrist while gathering a fistful from the nape of her neck in order to yank her head back until she was looking directly up at him, spittle dribbling from her mouth.

Noelle's mind went blank as she took in Krampus's

true form.

Outside, when she'd peeked at his beastly form through the tree branches, she'd had a vague notion that he was large, and terrifying, but Krampus was easily eight feet tall, his horns making him taller yet. She said a quick prayer of thanks that the brownstone had slanted, twelve-foot ceilings because there was no way he would fit in here, otherwise.

His upper body was like sculpted marble. Every muscle starkly defined, with pectorals the size of her head. Krampus's skin was dark as the night sky, with dazzling striations that appeared like glittering webs. His chiseled abdomen tapered off into fur, thick and black, that led down to his massive thighs and plate-sized hooves. Silver anklets made of bells twinkled in the dim light around his pasterns.

And between those ginormous thighs was a hefty erection, arcing up toward where a belly button would be on a man. It was easily the size of her wrist, with the base expanding to be near the width of her forearm, and Noelle was not delicately boned. The head was large and spear-shaped, different than the mushroom head of a human male's anatomy.

She wondered if she would get to experience the substantial width of him inside of her. The mere thought made her emit a whine as she peered up at Krampus from under her lashes. His burning crimson eyes were gazing back, feral, and unhinged.

His primal intensity sent chills throughout her body.

Without saying a word, he knotted her hair, weaving the rope that was previously tied around her chest through the knot He held onto the other end as he prowled around the table, keeping it taut so her head was forced back at an angle.

Despite having freed her upper body, Noelle's legs were still fastened to the table; her hips still dangling from an exposed rafter on the ceiling. She was still caught in his web of Christmas lights and ropes, with just a tad more freedom.

Noelle felt his fingers on her thighs, felt the claws slide away into something less damaging even as they retained their immense size. One hand was nearly large enough to cover her whole ass and her pussy clenched tightly at she imagined those digits inside of her.

Then, she didn't have to imagine anymore as a pair of knuckles stroked along her labia, pushing, and spreading the swollen flesh there. Rubbing in maddening strokes but never touching the one place she truly needed to be touched. He gathered a dollop of her wetness on his finger and stroked up to the pink whorl of her ass, caressing the sensitive nerves there. Noelle's hips flexed on instinct, seeking out more, as she mewled at the touch.

But instead of pushing deeper into that crevice,

he dragged the digit down as two fingers eased her cleft further apart so the button of her clitoris was fully exposed. She felt a tug at her the piercing, which made her jerk. Krampus pressed on the nub circling slowly, methodically, with the perfect amount of force.

Spasms of pleasure arcing through her core caused Noelle's legs to tremble. When she played with herself, her body always ached for faster movements, for the instant gratification of orgasm. She had never attempted this slow building of pleasure so intense it was nearly painful.

Ecstasy soared from that single, excruciatingly languid touch. It was an endless ascension—past the mountain top peak of her usual orgasms and into the sky, touching clouds of bliss previously unexplored. Her body jerked in stunted, aborted movements, hindered by the ropes around her lower extremities and knotted in her hair.

Deep, wailing cries poured from her lips as he meticulously wrecked her body with that circling of her clit. Her pussy was pulsating, tremors of delight pulling gushing fluids from her. Just as she was sure she could not handle the overwhelming pleasure any longer, she felt a warm, wet tickling against her hole.

He was lapping at her sopping cunt with his long, dexterous tongue.

A groan rumbled from Krampus's chest. "*Fuck*, pet.

You taste…" He ended the sentence by burying his face between her legs and feasting deeply from her.

Noelle's chest hitched as she shouted. Her head was swimming with bliss. She surrendered wholly to his ministrations, a slave to the pleasure he wrought. Passing out was a real possibility as she panted out desperate, gasping breaths as he brought her to orgasm repeatedly with that impossibly long tongue in her core and that teasing finger on her clit.

"God!" Noelle yelled, voice muffled, toes pointed and body clenched tight as another orgasm roared through her.

"Not quite godly, my pet, but I appreciate the sentiment," Krampus hummed against her quivering flesh.

"Please — hnng — no more. I can't take it," she attempted to beg around the gag, overcome. He appeared to understand her despite this.

"You can and you will," he replied, mercilessly in return.

Then his tongue moved up, slippery and teasing toward the tight, pinkened hole she rarely explored, and she wanted to tense up, wanted to slam her legs tightly shut, but couldn't due to the restraints. His tongue delved deep, diving into the snug cavity, and Noelle's breath caught at the sensation of it. Then she heard him spit before a wad of thick, warm saliva hit her directly there and a thumb rubbed it in.

As a finger started working into the hole, Krampus plugged her up with two more inside her cunt, hooking them in and pressing for the spongy part of her that made Noelle release deep, primal noises. Before long, he had worked her until she was relaxed and so deep into the pleasure that nearly all of his massive fist was being worked into her pussy while multiple fingers stretched her ass.

For a time, it was just this: the all-consuming joy of Krampus's fist within her, the gushing bliss he wrought from her body, and the animalistic cries she released. She drowned in ecstasy so deep she wasn't sure she would ever surface. It was a severe pleasure, unlike anything she had ever experienced before.

When she came down from another orgasm, reeling and foggy, she recognized that the thing in her ass now was no longer a finger, but something hard and unforgiving.

Metal? She thought.

At the same time, she also realized that her legs were unbound from the table and Krampus was rubbing her stiff muscles, much as he had her arms when he'd untied them. She groaned as she straightened her legs. Lactic acid had built up from disuse and her muscles burned at the renewed blood flow.

Krampus never said a word, just hummed as he

massaged her legs, from hips to knees, down to her ankles and even her feet. Digging deep into the arch, popping her toes, rotating her ankles, and going back up again until Noelle was a puddle of relaxed mush. Then, he helped her stand on wobbly legs, holding her steady until she could stand on her own power. He carefully unbuckled the gag, pulling the metal piece from between her teeth with a gentleness that surprised Noelle due to his size.

It was the first time she had been on her feet next to him and she was overwhelmed by how he dwarfed her. He was easily twice as tall as her. Noelle's chin came barely above his midriff and the enticing length of his cock was staring her nearly in the eye with a pearlescent drop of pre-come on the tip.

She leaned forward, enthralled, just wanting a lick, a mere taste, but a hand grabbed a fistful of hair at her scalp before her tongue made contact.

Krampus clicked his tongue at her. "No treats for trollops, pet."

A pout fit itself to her lips before she could stop it but he spotted it and released a gravelly laugh.

"Little bratty thing, you are. Never satisfied. Want to be stuffed full of my cock? Eat my cum down?" he asked this while one great big hand fisted that equally huge, erect cock. The other hand was still knotted in her hair, controlling the angle of her head, forcing her to look into his scarlet, goat-slitted eyes.

Noelle was so far gone, so deep into the happy, drugging haze of her mind, that all she was concerned about was pleasing him. Making Krampus happy. Making him come. So, she nodded her head as well as she could with the brutal grip he had on her hair and opened her mouth, small, red tongue poking out as she peered up at him from under her eyelashes.

Krampus loosed a sound from his cavernous chest that was somewhere between a purr and a growl. "Soon, so very soon, you'll get to swallow me down your throat." He bent at the waist, hooves shifting on the wooden floor as his large body angled deep enough that he could look her the eye. "But first, you take the switch."

CHAPTER FIVE

With an efficiency that spoke of years—centuries, Noelle mused—of practice, Krampus wrapped her wrists in thick leather cuffs before tossing a thick-linked chain with unerring accuracy over the exposed rafters. Once the chain settled, he grabbed both ends and, snatching up her wrists, pulled her hands high over her head, so high that she stood on her tiptoes. He secured her wrists to the chain.

He then went about attaching a metal pole, a spread bar he had called it, between her ankles further setting her off balance. A lot of her weight was on her wrists and shoulders, but not uncomfortably so. Finally, he worked on the metal hook that turned out to be inside her ass that was strung to a rope. He tugged the rope sharply, causing Noelle to gasp as he knotted the other end in her hair. With each jerk of her head, the rounded plug of the anal hook dug deeper inside her. The ornament hanging from her clit jingled with every move.

"Now, pet," started Krampus, stroking a hand down Noelle's side, grabbing at her thick hips as he went. "Your safe word is peppermint. Repeat it for me to show me you understand." Once she repeated it, he went through the purpose of safe words once more to ensure she understood and was cognizant of the situation even as lightheaded with arousal as she was.

Standing before her, Krampus fiddled with something in his colossal hand. When he reached her and started working her nipple to a hardened tip once more, Noelle had a good idea as to what he cradled. His long tongue snaked out, wrapping around one nipple, soaking it, while his fingers pinched and pulled at the other. He worked her right breast, massaging it, flicking the pebbled tip, pulling it taut. His claws dug in so deep they left bloodied scratches that made her cry out.

Krampus licked the blood from her chest as it dripped between the valley of her breasts.

Holding the right nipple tightly, he held out one clamp and let the teeth of it shut around the extended tip before he let go, dropping the nipple and the heavy, metal clamp.

"Fuck!" Noelle shouted, body shuddering with the sharp bite of pain. As she jerked, the anal hook tugged at her ass, making her throw her head back to get some release from the deep pressure.

There was nowhere to go — she was trapped by pain on both ends.

"Shhh," Krampus soothed, rubbing her left nipple, preparing it for the clamp. Her chest heaved. "Remember how to get out of this if you can't take it?"

Noelle nodded frantically. She remembered, she did. But she could handle this.

Biting her lip, she watched as he drew out her other nipple between two claws and closed the clamp around it. She arched her back against the flood of pain even as wetness seeped from her core. Noelle breathed into the hurt, groaning deep in her chest on her exhalations.

As he had before, Krampus stopped touching her and let her stew in the anticipation as the fog of subspace built up heavier inside her mind.

The only lighting in the room was a multi-colored string of Christmas lights he had used to wrap her up like a Christmas tree beforehand and the faint flickering of the false flames of her electric fireplace in the living room. It was quiet, save for her panting breaths and the sound of his massive hooves thumping on the floor as he moved around her. Noelle wondered if his preternatural ears could hear the blood thundering through her veins, pumping into her pounding heart, making her aching clit pulsate.

Suddenly, a whistling sound in the air and then fire licked up the back of her thighs from where he struck her. Pain so brutally intense she could choke on it. It locked her body up, the agony so acute she froze in place, unable to utter a sound.

The second strike landed before she had recovered from the first and the shock of pain registered through her. Noelle could nearly feel the skin beneath the strikes blooming into welts, could almost sense the blood rushing to the spots to heal the damage incurred.

It was a heady sensation, being so in tune with your body even as you pushed it to its limits.

The hissing whistle sounded again and another blow — this time on the seat of her ass and she tried to drop her head to absorb the pain, to just breathe through it, but the sharp tug in her ass reminded her she couldn't.

"No," Noelle suddenly said. "No, please. No, no, no." She was chanting it even as she prepared herself for the next hit.

Because no didn't mean stop. Noelle knew what her safe word was and while she was on the edge of her limit, she wasn't prepared to use it yet even as body and mind fought against the hurt.

Two more precise, lethal strikes landed in an x across her rump and then Krampus was cradling her close, cooing to her, "What a good girl you are. Such a good girl for me."

Noelle was sobbing, her head buzzing. Desperate heaving breaths exiting her as she shook and shuddered in his arms. As her body expelled the tension and adrenaline, she realized the buzzing sound she heard wasn't just in her head but was in fact a vibrator that Krampus had apparently summoned from midair. He pressed the humming toy against the metal hook and she shouted at the pleasurable sensation.

"There you go, pet. Let me make you feel good," he purred in her ear. "I want you to come on my hand, and then around my cock." He began stroking her clit with two fingers. Circling it round and round, dipping lower to gather some of her of dripping wetness, before sliding back up to rub her harder. He had a precise rhythm, a fast pace with hard pressure that, combined with the echoing vibrations, was sure to set her off quickly.

Moaning loudly, she rotated her hips as best as she could against his fingers, feeling the plugged hook deep in her ass with each move. The vibrations lit up her spine and resonated through her cunt. Within minutes, she was back on the edge of release. Noelle wasn't sure how this man could get her body prepared for an orgasm so quickly.

While she could get herself off in under five minutes, it usually took partners fifteen plus minutes of foreplay to get Noelle primed and relaxed enough before she was even considering climbing the peak to happy fun time. And after one orgasm, she was done and over with, almost like her body said — that's it, buddy. Time's up.

But Krampus? He'd wrung numerous climaxes out of her and her vagina was still weeping happily for him.

As she teetered at the edge of another, Noelle turned her head, her tear-stained eyes trying to meet Krampus's. He tilted his head down for her and gave her a dirty, fanged smirk before biting his lip as his eyes then skimmed down the front of her body to watch his hand play with her pussy.

"You're soaking wet for me still, Noelle. I love your sopping cunt." Hearing those filthy words in his gravelly voice made her legs tremble almost as much the magic his hand was performing. His head dipped down and he bit along her neck, tongue flicking out to tease her earlobe.

"Please, please," she begged, unsure exactly what she was begging for. She wanted to kiss him, she wanted to come. She wanted to writhe on his dick and gush her pleasure for him.

"Look at you, begging so pretty. What do you need, pet?" Krampus asked, tone like gravel. She could feel his erection, heavy and hot, digging into her upper back.

"Kiss me," Noelle pleaded around a moan. "Please."

"So much I would give you right now and you ask for a thing so simple." He let out an incredulous huff of laughter, shaking his head. White locks of hair shook and the bells tangled in the strands jingled. Then he swooped down, claiming her lips with his.

He dominated her with that kiss; stole her breath directly from her lungs.

It was fangs against teeth, bruising in its intensity and when his tongue touched hers, he ate her moan from her mouth as she came against his hand. Noelle's hips bucked hard even as she tried to stay still so she could keep her lips attached to his. His breath was minty sweet, like a candy cane, and this close, he smelled like an evergreen tree covered in snow — something earthy and cold.

As he pulled back from her, a line of spit connected them and he licked it away with his abnormally long tongue.

"You kiss like you need it to survive," Krampus breathed, crimson clashing with her garland-green eyes.

"I've never met anyone that kisses me like you do," she whispered in return, honesty falling from her lips like crumbs from a cake. He cradled her face in his hand, leaning forward to press a kiss to her forehead.

"Let's get you untied. And then…" he paused as he eyed her.

"And then?" she asked, wary.

"I want you to choke on my cock," he finished, voice darkening.

"Please," Noelle whimpered.

After Krampus had unhooked Noelle from the ceiling and unleashed her legs from the spread bar, he gathered her in his arms and carried her to the living room. He settled her on the emerald colored, velvet couch, nipple clamps and cunt ornament still firmly in place before he covered her with a blanket and went to grab her a glass of water. Once he ensured that she drank the whole glass down, he took the glass from her hand and placed it on the golden, mid-century modern side table.

"Before we continue," Krampus started, kneeling before her, hands on either side of her hips. "I want you to know that your punishment is complete. You are not obligated to give me any pleasure. Do you understand?"

Noelle nodded, confused.

"You don't want to have sex?" she inquired, slightly hurt. She had hoped this whole thing would culminate in them hurtling their bodies at one another.

But Krampus shook his head. He reached out,

placing a finger under her chin so he could look her directly in the eye. "You misunderstand, pet. I want nothing more to lose myself in your body. To sink my cock so deep inside you that you'll think of me for weeks because of the ache. But I want to be sure that you want it and don't think you're forced to have sex with me."

"I want it," she breathed, tongue dipping out to wet her suddenly dry lips. "God, I want it so bad."

Krampus's thumb traced her lips before dragging her bottom lip down. She poked her tongue out and swirled it around his thumb, careful of his claw.

He growled, "You tempt me like no other creature ever has."

"Good," Noelle murmured back, breath getting heavy as she took his thumb into her mouth. Despite the numerous orgasms, her body was coming alive again. Heating back up at the idea of him inside of her — in her mouth, in her pussy — spreading her wide open. Out of the corner of her eye, she could see his erection. It had been flaccid earlier having flagged between the earlier activities and stopping to grab her a drink and ensure she was an active participant in their encounter, but it was thickening right before her eyes as she sucked on his thumb.

Suddenly surging to his feet, he proclaimed, "Enough teasing. I want your mouth on my cock.

Remember your safe word hand signal?" At my nod, he continued. "Good, because you won't be able to speak for a long time."

With that, he grabbed double fistfuls of her candy-cane red hair and led her down to his dark, weeping erection.

CHAPTER SIX

His flavor burst over Noelle's tongue at the same time his musky scent encased her. She had a lot of friends that complained about the odor and taste of dick, but she loved the primal aroma. It was heady, intoxicating. The sweat, the earthy musk — there was nothing like it.

He had no hair, just fur at the base of his cock. Noelle wanted to bury her face in it so she did, inhaling deeply; she moaned, looking up at him as her chin rested low on his pelvis. Krampus was staring down at her, eyes like twin flames in the darkness of the room.

Keeping her eyes on him she licked down the shaft, gathering spit on her tongue and forcing it onto the huge length as she traveled down it. Her hand encircled him, her fingers inches from meeting, and worked Krampus's cock, using her spit as lube. A rumble sounded from his chest that she felt vibrating through his body more than she heard.

When she reached the flared head, she licked deep into the slit, causing his hands to fist tighter in her hair as he hissed out a breath. Noelle laughed, feeling coquettish, and then swallowed down the tip of his cock, suckling on it.

Krampus groaned above her.

Glancing up through her lashes, she gazed at him as his head fell back, white hair fanning out across his coal-black shoulders. His pecs and abs were bunched up, tight with strain. The deep line between his abs and v lining his hips was mouthwatering. She moaned her appreciation.

"Open your mouth wide for me, pet." Krampus grabbed her by the skull in his huge hands and shifted his hooves on the floor to get better footing. "Be a good girl and let me fuck your face."

Noelle opened her mouth wide, tongue out to cover her bottom teeth.

"Gonna choke you up real fucking good," he said, his accent going rough. "Gag you with my cock."

Nodding, Noelle moaned just before Krampus rammed his cock inside her mouth, so rough she gagged on impact. He backed up far enough for her to take a breath and then shoved back in, forcing himself far enough back that he touched the back of her throat.

Noelle's hands came up in panic as her body fought against the intrusion. She placed them on his corded thighs, clenching in the thick fur.

Her eyes watered as she gagged, throat retching against the wide head of him. He cradled her skull deeper as he angled his knees, forcing himself even deeper. Every muscle in her body worked to expel him. Finally, right as Noelle worried she would lose the contents of her stomach, he pulled back and she inhaled a gasping breath, coughing.

Tears were streaming down her eyes and drool stained her chin as she gazed up at him in adoration.

"That's right, my sweet pet. Take it," he hissed, shoving back inside.

Krampus set a brutal pace, slamming himself into her throat over and over again. Every gag she released appeared to spur him on. Finally, he released a roar, bellowing his release to the sky as he came in huge, jerking pumps down Noelle's throat. There was so much salty cum flowing from his cock that she couldn't swallow it down fast it enough. It dribbled from her mouth and onto her breasts.

Sated for the moment, he dragged his dick from her mouth before slapping her across the cheek with it.

Noelle just moaned in return. She felt hazy, drugged up on arousal. She reached out for him, but he just grabbed her wrists together in one huge hand and made her lean back on the couch.

With her hands behind her head in his grasp, her tits were nearly in his face and he took the opportunity to remove the nipple clamps. As sensation suddenly came back to her nipple, Noelle gasped.

"*Fuck*," she cursed, groaning.

"Endorphins," Krampus said knowingly, a dark smile in his voice. He removed the second clamp, sending Noelle spiraling again. "Grab your knees for me. Hold your legs up."

She did what he asked, twitching as his knuckle grazed her overused clit. "I love your pretty cunt. Gets sopping wet for me." Noelle felt a light tug on the hood of her clit and saw the ornament be placed on the side table. "Show me your slit, pet. Hold yourself open for me."

Arms still under her knees, Noelle crunched up deeper, nearly curling herself in half to reach her fingers down to her pussy. She spread her labia apart, letting him take in her aroused cunt. She could feel it clenching and unclenching beneath his stare, could feel the slide of slick as it oozed out of her.

"Fucking delicious cunt," he growled. "So swollen for me, so ready for my cock."

"Yes, yes, please," Noelle cried out, hips moving of their own accord as she imagined his dick diving into her.

He lurched over her, clawed hands on the back of the couch as his massive body settled over hers. One furred knee settled on the couch, and she heard the furniture groan beneath his weight. His prick settled against her slit and she trembled at the length of him.

"You took my fist earlier. You can take my cock. Are you ready?" Krampus asked, rubbing his cock in her wetness, glancing it off her clit.

"Fuck me," she pleaded. "Fuck me, fuck me, fuck me."

On the last word, he thrust forward, forcing himself in. Noelle squealed, body lurching at the strength behind his charge. He was wide, so wide her pussy strained around him. By his third thrust, Noelle had lost control of the ability to hold her legs up and wrapped them around his lean waist as her arms arced back, hand clenching tightly onto the sofa.

She gasped as he owned her pussy with his endless cock, thighs shaking violently from where they were hooked around his hips.

"You're so tight, pet. I wish you could see how pretty you look locked around me." Krampus fucked into her slowly, still allowing her to get used to his ungodly size.

As her moans increased in frequency, he quickened his pace, hips thrusting with a brutal pressure. He fucked her as if it were a punishment and she wanted to accept it all.

With Krampus, she had discovered a form of freedom in the loss of her inhibitions. She could leave her reservations and anxiety at the door because when she was with Krampus, he was in charge. But even at his most domineering, he never crossed the line into controlling. Never got to a point where Noelle felt scared or intimidated by him, despite his size.

She reveled in this night of release.

Rocking her hips sharply, Noelle fucked herself stupid on Krampus' giant cock. She cried out each time the flared head scraped against her g-spot perfectly.

"Rub your clit. Make yourself come on my cock," he hissed. His eyes were flaring brightly in the dim room, his teeth flashing white as he snarled in pleasure.

Reaching down, Noelle frantically circled her clit. Her pussy was sopping wet, it was squelching out of her with every fuck of his cock into her tight passage. There was zero friction for circling so she switched it up, just rubbing two fingers over the hood of her clit to get traction. Pleasure zinged from her clit and through out her body.

Krampus's eyes were focused on where they were joined. "That's it, my good girl. Strumming that clit so nice." He panted for moment, seemingly overcome. "I wish you could see how we fit together. You're stretched so tightly around me, so pretty and pink."

Noelle could feel her orgasm building. It glittered at the edge of her version as bone deep pleasure ached in her stomach.

"Oh god, almost," she wailed. Keening moans were escaping her mouth with embarrassing frequency. Krampus leaned down and swallowed them from her mouth.

Whole body clenched up tight, Noelle screamed as she came, her tight cunt milking Krampus's release from him as he bellowed above her. Inside her, she felt him spurting in copious bursts and then a weird tickling, like his dick had sprung appendages. They pressed deep against her cervix, pressing and massaging, sending her into a richer, more intense orgasm; one she had never felt before.

Overwhelmed, Noelle took one last great big gasping breath, before passing out.

"Wake up, pet. Drink some water and eat a cookie for me."

Krampus's deep voice roused Noelle. Groggily, she sat up, freezing when her body ached.

"Ow," she moaned pathetically.

"Yes, very ow," Krampus agreed. He was sitting beside her on her bed, fully dressed. "You're going to be very ow for a few days. Since you sleep like the dead,

I went ahead and rubbed you down with some arnica cream to help alleviate some of the pain."

He pushed a glass of water into her hands. "Now, drink all of this for me." Once she had, he handed her two chocolate chip cookies, which she nibbled on, enjoying the rich chocolate. As she was licking the last crumb from her fingers, Krampus had come back from where he disappeared into her bathroom, and came baring her toothpaste, sodden with a dollop of toothpaste.

"Time to clean your teeth, pet." Krampus watched her intently as she brushed her teeth, before holding out the empty glass that had previously held her water so she could spit. After rinsing the cup and letting her swish her mouth clean, he replaced the toothbrush back at the sink and came back brandishing a brush.

"Hair," he proclaimed this time, but instead of handing the brush to her, he gripped the wooden handle tightly and began running the brush through her long strands. Anytime he came across a knot, he worked it out gently, until her hair was smooth and gleaming in the moonlight shining through the windows.

At this point, sleep was tugging at Noelle's eyelids so hard she could barely keep them open so as he walked the hairbrush back to the bathroom, she slid back under the covers, nestling in deep.

Noelle thought Krampus might have kissed her

forehead, but she wasn't sure if that was real or a dream as she was already fast asleep before he came back into the room.

CHAPTER SEVEN

Christmas morning dawned, bright and cheery, matching Noelle's mood perfectly.

Her body was bruised and ached in places she wasn't aware that bodies could ache in. She stretched, flannel sheets rubbing deliciously against her naked skin, relishing in the blossom of hurt that grew. Noelle had never considered herself much of a masochist before last night, but something about pushing her boundaries to the limits, testing her pain threshold, had really done it for her.

She wondered how bad she would have to be this year to have a repeat visit from Krampus and immediately began plotting dastardly deeds.

Grinning to herself, she covered her face with her comforter and let out a squeal of delight, feet kicking under her duvet.

I have a crush on Krampus! She thought incredulously.

But who could blame her! He was debonair and suave. Handsome in both his human and monster form, and he fucked like a beast. Noelle pressed her thighs together, feeling the ache of him.

A tingle of arousal shot through her body. "Down girl," she scolded her vagina. "He's gone. We have to remain calm."

Noelle sat up, groaning as her body resisted the movement. On her bedside table, she spotted pain medicine and a glass of water as well as a note. In neat, precise handwriting, it stated, "Be a good girl and swallow these for me." There was no signature but there didn't need to be.

After taking the medicine, she slid from the bed and hobbled to the shower. Once it was running and steam was filling the bathroom, she took in her appearance, eyes lighting upon all the marks and bruises on her pale skin. Turning around, she gasped at the purple welts along her backside and thighs from the switch. She ran a hand over them, flinching. The flesh was tender to the touch, the skin knotted and ridged.

But even as she remembered the pain of the switch, her pussy clenched at the reminder of the pleasure that followed. Placing a hand against the wall, Noelle kept her eyes trained on the darkened flesh as she brought one hand down to her clit, rubbing it frantically as she relived her night with Gus von Krampus.

The sounds of the shower couldn't drown out her hisses of pleasure as she brought herself to orgasm twice with the rapid rotation of her fingers. Finally, she forced her fingers away from her throbbing clit.

"Christ," she cursed as her legs trembled with aftershocks.

Noelle was a little concerned she was hooked on Krampus.

She showered quickly, forgoing blow drying her hair for the option of French braiding the long red tresses in a crown around her head. After brushing her teeth, she slathered on gingerbread smelling lotion, inhaling the cinnamon fragrance, before tugging on sleek black leggings and a thigh-length emerald sweater. She stuffed her feet into fluffy grey socks and deemed herself company ready.

In the kitchen, she munched on an apple as she put cinnamon rolls in the oven and brewed a fresh pot of coffee.

Every year for Christmas, her friend Yule would come over and they would watch classic Christmas movies, get wine drunk, and eat their weight in cheese and sweets. Usually, Noelle's apartment with Craig was already decorated prior to Christmas day, so she would have to scramble today to get everything done before Yule showed up this afternoon.

The coffee maker beeped, alerting Noelle that the bean juice of life was finished brewing, and she grabbed the pot and her favorite mug before pouring herself a glass. She poured in peppermint mocha creamer, inhaling the rich minty scent, before taking a sip. Noelle moaned at the flavor.

That first sip of coffee in the morning was heavenly.

As she meandered to the living room to finish putting up décor, she peeked into the formal dining room. To her surprise, there was no mess. Beyond that, Krampus had apparently decorated this room for her. Thick greenery draped along the rafters, with holly berries interspersed throughout. A huge wreath with pinecones was centered on the wall by the head of table. In the center of the table sat an elegant piece of greenery made up of evergreen boughs, pinecones, and flameless, electric candles.

No fire hazard, Noelle thought, amused.

On the sleek credenza against the opposite wall were numerous wire-wrapped golden trees of varying heights, sparkling in the light peeking through the blinds. Fairy lights were interwoven into garland, which was snaked around the gilded trees.

The room was stunning. A beautiful, eclectic mix of natural and modern. Flawlessly her style.

Noelle swung around, carefully cradling the coffee mug as she headed toward the living room and…yes.

This room too. Krampus had decorated it.

Smiling, Noelle took it in.

The same thick garland from the dining room lined the curtain rods above her burgundy velvet curtains. Her mantle was draped in a chain of dried orange slices and cinnamon pieces. Ivory candles sat on it, fake flames flickering.

Her tree — that *fucking pesky* tree — was lit up in with multicolor lights. Gold ornaments of contrasting sizes draped across the branches. Ornate ribbon flowed down the tree in elegant waves. A massive golden bow sat at the top, imperial. At the floor was a single present. A black box tied up with a green bow.

Before she could check it out, the oven timer chimed, forcing her back into the kitchen. As she pulled the cinnamon rolls out of the oven, she mulled over the gift.

Krampus wouldn't have gotten her a present… right? He had punished thousands of people over his lifetime…surely, she wasn't any different, despite her wish to be.

She gnawed on her lip, attempting to ignore the urgency in her veins to open that package.

"I'm going to drink my coffee, slowly, and then I'll open it," she told herself, bringing her mug to her lips.

Her best laid plan went haywire, because the moment the liquid touched her mouth, she was chugging the caffeine down with lightning quick speed.

"Would you look at that, all done." Noelle chucked her mug into the sink and ran down the hall, skidding on her socks as she turned the corner to her living room.

Crashing to her knees, she took a deep breath and carefully undid the green ribbon. It unraveled slowly and fluttered to the ground. Closing her eyes, she opened the lid of the box. When nothing happened, she peeked open an eye.

Inside, sat a card.

"What the fuck?" Noelle queried aloud.

Dipping a hand inside, she brought the card out for closer inspection. On it, in simple black ink, was a number. No name, nothing else. Just ten digits.

Did he… *gift* her his phone number?

One: conceited.

Two: *oh my god*.

Heart fluttering, Noelle raced back to her bedroom, breath huffing as she took the stairs two at a time. Grabbing her phone, she dialed in the number before making herself wait. She couldn't call him and sound like she was half dead.

When her breath was mostly back to normal, she hit call. She waited in breathless anticipation as the phone rang.

Finally, a click. And then: "Hello, pet. Merry Christmas."

Acknowledgements

Phew. Somebody smoke a cigarette for me and hand the bourbon, I need a break after that sexplosion!

Fucking Amy Briggs, for being the real MVP. I owe you my second born and every cat in the world.

AJ Wolf, for being a BAMF and having my back last minute.

Julia Murray, for always hyping me up and not being mad at me when I'm like SURPISE.

Sam Coleman, for reading this baby when I panic-messaged her and was like, "DO YOU MIND" after I scrapped the first ending and beta'd it for me.

My Street Team, for their hard work and all their support.

My ARC Team, for always being willing to read whatever I throw at them.

My readers, thank you for all that you do for me! Every page read, every review—it all counts and it means so, so much to me.

THE
MURDER
GAME

"Ooh," I moaned. "Is that what you want? Wanna watch me come on my fingers?" I circled my clit with two fingers, black panties tugged to the side of my bare mound as I faced the camera. Three fingers from my other hand dipped in and out of my sopping hole, squelching loudly in the empty room. My legs were carelessly thrown over the arms of the chair, giving my audience an uninterrupted view of me. A shiver worked its way up my spine as my core heated even more and my juices slid down my hand. Tossing my head back, I hissed at the pleasure.

A ping sounded as my followers typed in their requests. I let out a sultry giggle as I read them, grabbing a vibrator that was on standby on my desk. "Got your gift right here, honey. Thanks for sending it to me."

My silver hair slid over my bare shoulders as I adjusted my position, completely removing my lacy thong and stuffing it between my red lips as a viewer requested. I moaned lasciviously around the cloth between my teeth, voice high pitched. It was my acting voice, my fake moan — but the customers loved it. I tended to be quiet during sex, so all this noise? Purely for my viewers.

Turning the vibrator on the lowest setting, I set it just above my clit, rotating it in small circles. I breathed into the new feeling of pleasure, my keen muffled from the thong. Pulling my wet fingers from my cunt, I plucked at my nipples before grabbing deeper at my breasts, taking handfuls, and digging my nails into the skin. I pressed hard enough to bruise. One handed, I clicked the vibrator onto a higher setting, spreading my legs wider and making faster circles as the buzzing ate away at my nerves.

My first orgasm was building quickly. I pointed my toes, tensing my thighs and calves, holding my breath as I felt it approach. Then I backed the vibrator off. Body shaking with the loss of near ecstasy, I laughed at the rapid-fire of pings, indicating more messages. I read them over quickly as I used fingers to softly stroke myself down from the edge, hips twitching.

"Mmm," I groaned, arching my back, offering my chest up for a better view as I dipped the vibrator into my clenching, aching pussy. It had a bulbous end and was curved, perfect for hitting that angled spot right at the front of me. Switching it back on, I started thrusting it in and out, striving for that spot. Hitching my leg up under my elbow, the fingers of that hand strummed my clit quickly. Hips moving, I gyrated in the chair, arching against my own hands.

There was nothing better than this; nothing more beautiful than bringing pleasure to yourself. And nothing got me hotter than knowing I was doing it in front of an audience that got off on my pleasure. I always loved being the center of attention, but this took it to a whole 'nother level.

In my fucked up little adopted family, Chamberlain got all the attention — not that he wanted it, either — but here, now, everyone had their eyes on me.

Everyone wanted me.

"Fuck, fuck, fuck," I whined, voice hushed by the thong in my mouth. Because the cloth was drying, my mouth was producing more spit, and it was starting to drool around the edges of my mouth, and I let it. My head thrashed back and forth as the tip of the vibrator struck my g-spot repeatedly, my legs beginning to wobble as a tremor built in them.

A steady bray of "huh huh huh" breaths belted out of me as my orgasm grew nearer and glitter lined the edges of my vision. Eyes snapping closed, my whole body went taut. I yanked the vibrator out just in time for a gush of liquid to squirt out, hips jerking, thighs quaking, pussy making an absolute mess of my chair as I yelled out my joy.

I collapsed back into my chair, hand automatically reaching up to brush my hair back before remembering I was wearing the mask I always did during my online performances. I settled for leaning my head on my hand, tugging the thong loose from my mouth with the other as I smiled. I was sure my lip stick was smeared around my mouth from the drool, and I loved it.

Sex shouldn't be clean; it should be messy, sticky,

absolutely filthy.

The smile I gave my viewers spoke of my love of grime and filth; it was pure cat got the canary satisfaction. I bid them farewell, telling them I'd see them next week before shutting off my camera. I left the chat up so that I could tell the remaining viewers bye before I shut down my laptop, but MorgueDoll was done for the day and now I was back to being Priestly King as I slipped the black, nylon half mask off my face with a happy sigh.

Body sated, I collapsed onto my bed, running my hands over my tingling skin, through the wetness staining my thighs. Which reminded me—I needed to wipe up the mess I'd made.

As I used a towel and cleaning spray to wipe up my desk and chair, I heard shouting voices, and what sounded like a stampede of elephants coming down the hallway. I rolled my eyes, knowing Chamberlain and his cronies were here. Even as I snarked about them in my mind, a smile played at the edge of my lips.

I'd grown up with Lain and his two best friends—Camber Ashford and Atley Dodge—and most of my childhood was filled with their teasing… but also their protection.

Those three never let another kid so much as tug on a strand of my hair without getting a wallop from their fists. Being surrounded by three lion-fierce protectors had made dating difficult during my adolescence until they'd left for college three years ago. Now, in their senior year at Eddington U, I'd had my share of dating without their interference.

But my body still lit up anytime I saw Chamberlain and his friends.

I always tried to fight it — he was my adopted brother, dammit — but so much of my childhood revolved around him. My happiest memories are filled with him. Those three swooped into my life like dark avenging angels, scaring back the darkness and teaching me the most important lesson of my life: how to be happy.

Getting older meant growing apart from them, but they always spared a few days of summer break for me. Chamberlain barely spared a glance for me most holidays, but Camber and Atley still treated me like the little sister they never had, and I ate up their attention. I had started to worry they wouldn't have time to visit me this summer until I heard them thunder up the stairs.

I contemplated washing the stench of sex from me, but I realized I wanted them to smell it on me. I wanted them to see me as something other than the broken little kid they used to protect. I was 18 now, and I'd be joining them at Eddington this August.

After wiping the smeared lipstick off my mouth, I

dressed in a pair of grey joggers that Chamberlain had outgrown years ago and slipped a cropped sweatshirt on over my bare chest. It showed off my tight stomach and pierced belly button as I rolled up the band of the joggers to a better length. They were still overly long, but unbelievably comfortably with wear and age. My cherry-red toenails peeked out from the bottom and I wiggled them, my toe rings glinting in the lights. I yanked the twin braids out of my hair, throwing my shoulder-length silver strands up into a messy bun. Grabbing my deodorant, I swiped a few times under my arms before capping it — I wanted to smell like sex, not stink.

Swiping my phone off the dresser, I checked my messages as I exited my room. My best friend, Sawyer, had texted me about a huge end-of-summer bash she was attending, and would I be wing man?! Smiling, I messaged her back with a big fuck yeah as I knocked on Chamberlain's door. I heard the grumble of his voice and opened it wide, smirking as the boys all turned in my direction.

Atley was the closest to the door, lounging in Lain's desk chair. He was a hulking beast of a man; muscular, yes, but mostly just the sheer size of him was overwhelming. Atley soared over six feet tall, closer to seven feet than anything else. His body dwarfed the chair he sat in, legs spread wide, eating up the space in front of him.

I bit my lip as I took him in.

Dark brown hair with ombre-blonde tips tumbled over his brow, nearly obscuring his glazed hazel eyes. His nose was slightly crooked, something that had changed since I'd last seen him. A constellation of freckles sat over his cheeks, barely visible against his summer tan. He smiled at me, and it was hazy.

Atley was hiding from himself. In the smoke of his weed and the fog of his pills, Atley could drown out the intrusive thoughts that invaded his mind, never giving him peace. His parents refused to allow him to attend therapy because the Dodge children were perfect with a capital P. So, it fell back on Atley to fix himself, and amid finding his cure, he was slowly dying in the ruin of his mind.

Hand snaking out, Atley grasped the front of my sweatshirt, dragging me down into his lap. I laughed as he did it, soaking up the attention as my back rested against the curve of his arm, both of my legs draped over his, so I sat against him sideways. His nose nuzzled my neck and I heard him sniff as it traced from my shoulder up to my ear.

"Little saint, you don't smell so innocent today," his deep voice grumbled. "You smell more like a sinner. What have you been up to?" A dark smile laced his words. He nipped my ear and I laughed, slapping his chest with my hand.

"Stop teasing her, Dodge," came Camber's voice from my right. "Don't act like you weren't dipping your dick into the samplings at the hotel this morning." I turned my head to take Camber in. His voice was monotone, even. Surprisingly deeper than Atley's even though Camber lacked his height. But what he lacked in stature, he made up for in genius. Camber was the brilliant one of the group; he went along with the shenanigans of the other two, but he always had an air of superiority about him like he thought the actions were juvenile. Despite that, Camber was the good one. He had a smile for strangers he crossed paths with and offered a helping hand to those in need. But under that carefully crafted smile was the shadowed edge of darkness. You could see it peeking out from time to time if you paid attention.

That darkness was staring at me now as he looked down his nose at me, cave-dark eyes gleaming behind his glasses. His dirty blonde hair was juxtaposed by the rest of him — it was artfully messy, tufts sticking up here and there, while the rest of his outfit was neatly pressed, right down to the slacks he wore. Camber was always impeccably dressed. All the years I'd known Camber, I'd never seen him in jeans and only in sleep pants once, when a girl at a party had spilled red wine on his pants and I'd offered to wash them for him.

Atley harrumphed behind me. "Maybe you'd lose that stick up your ass if you'd 'dip your dick' a little more, asshole."

Not even deigning to roll his eyes, Camber's steady, intense gaze never left mine. It was like a game of chicken—whoever looked away first lost. His head titled back more at a more imperial angle, eyes narrowing, and it took everything in me to not wilt under his forceful stare even as my body heated. I shifted in Atley's lap and his huge hand palmed my hip, taking up my whole side as his fingers spanned from hip bone to rib. A sly grin ate away the smile previously resting on my face and I felt the cunning curve of it as it slid into place. I enjoyed the power of this grin; it was one I wore when I was MorgueDoll—fully in control of my audience as they panted for me.

And Camber still didn't flinch. If anything, the hardness of his features settled deeper, knife-edge sharp as he waited for me to stand down from our staring contest. His head titled to the side, animal-like, and his mouth parted; that full bottom lip pouting open. He stroked it with a finger and that damned finger is what did me in. I glanced at it for a split second and it cost me.

His face never changed—no smile, no outwardly show of pleasure at my loss, but deep satisfaction shown in the fathomless depths of his eyes as I huffed, crossing my arms over my chest.

Pulled from the sway of Camber's stare, Atley's voice filtered back in and I realized he was having a conversation with Chamberlain, the last member of this motley crew. Canting my head just so, I peeked at my brother from the corner of my eyes.

Chamberlain was the epitome of what the St Claire heir should look like. His face was charming, beautiful, with a classic roman nose and patrician features enviable by those who go under the knife to perfect their facial structures. Tousled brown hair, deep navy eyes, sun-kissed skin, and an accent that comes with wealth and good breeding. Everything that made up Chamberlain suggested gallantry and control.

But underneath that perfect shell lay the true Chamberlain, the one living beneath the ideal that comes with being a St Claire. When he glides into a suit, he's charming and slippery; able to coerce the stodgiest of businessmen into deals even as he persuaded their wives to slip down his zipper under the table. This form of Chamberlain's was a porcelain doll and like all dolls, he was carved out by the hands that crafted him — and his creators were cruel. He played his role as dutiful son perfectly, even if the job destroyed him.

Out of the suit, he was passionate, unsettled; dark tattoos lined almost every inch of him as he craved to have the armor of his skin match the nightmares in his mind. This version of Chamberlain stared at the world with an aching desperation, his eyes radiating such fevered intensity that he reminded me of a starving animal. Feral. Unpredictable. Deadly.

Chamberlain was staring back me even as his conversation with Atley continued. I sucked in a breath, biting my lip as my body stiffened. Atley's hand clenched against my waist tighter, seemingly without notice, but Chamberlain's eyes flickered to the large, tanned fingers touching the bare skin above his old joggers before flicking back to hold my gaze.

I wondered what he remembered. Wondered if he ever thought of it, of me. Ever missed it, like I did.

I squirmed in Atley's lap, unsettled. Atley's head leaned down and I smelled the sun on his skin as he whispered in my ear, "Be still, little girl. I'm not as pure as those two when it comes to you." I knew he meant Camber and Chamberlain, who always kept me at an arm's length away while Atley tugged me close. "Wriggle much more and you'll find yourself writhing on my dick." He nipped my neck with the last of his words and I gasped, shoving at his chest, but not hard enough to move him. Atley just gave a dark chuckle.

"How was your summer, sister?" Chamberlain's voice was smoke and bourbon, dark. Honeyed. So thick I could almost taste the vowels he spoke in the air. I was desperate for any part of him that he offered to me, even just five measly words.

Turning to face him, I braced myself before meeting his endlessly blue eyes again. "Decent. Mom wanted to go to Paris again, so we went for a month. Dad stayed behind, as usual. Work stuff. Other than that, I was with Sawyer most of the time."

"Ooh, yeah, that hot little friend of yours. I miss seeing her around. Gotta say I love watching her go more than anything, though." Atley said, and even Camber huffed out a small chuckle at that.

"Pig," I groused, but I was smiling. Sawyer had a great ass and everyone knew it.

"You know it, baby," the pig in question agreed, taking the insult in stride. I had no doubt he'd been called worse when he'd undoubtedly broken some poor girl's heart, because these three? They had a reputation for staying for a night and never visiting again.

I think every girl in school hoped they'd have the magic snatch that would reel them in for keeps, but it never worked. Didn't stop them from trying and subsequently getting heartbroken afterward, though, even after knowing the boys' reputation.

I think that's part of the reason why I was addicted to being in their presence. It was almost like a high. I got to spend time with them, got to see them in ways no one else did because of my connection to Chamberlain. I've seen them at the lowest points in life; been there to help console them when family members had passed, or bad shit inevitability went down with their parents. As much as they had taught me to be happy, they had also taught me the importance of connection. And the four of us? We had a tight connection.

Even if it felt like it had frayed some this summer during their long absence.

Laying my head against Atley's chest, I listened to the heavy, steady thumping of his heart under my ear and soaked up the warmth of his skin. Before I knew it, I was drifting off to sleep, comforted by the presence of my boys and Atley's hand stroking my hair.

Chapter One

*I*t was the dream that woke me.

I sensed the vestiges dwelling in the back of my mind but was unable to remember the details. It was akin to a sepia photograph burdened by time, barely visible in my mind's eye. Of everything, the mood lingered most, festering beneath my skin. An ache of fear haunted my bones while ghostly tendrils of the adrenaline rush I'd experienced had my heart fluttering like a trapped bird behind its bone cage.

Something horrible occurred in the dream.

Not knowing what haunted my sleeping self was beginning to have its toll on me. A dull throb pulsated behind my eyelids threatening to become a full-fledged migraine. Rolling over, I tugged my quilt higher and nestled my nose into it. It smelled of lavender and lemon balm; our mother—my twin's and mine—was a proponent of aromatherapy and regularly brewed droughts to spray on our bedding to aid us in sleep. Despite it, I was unable to fall back asleep.

A quiet voice, rough with sleep, whispered, "Ezra, c'mere." Shuffling noises came from the other side of our shared room.

Noa, my sister.

Smiling faintly, I rose from my bed and tiptoed to hers, stealthily avoiding the wooden slats I knew creaked, so as not to awaken our mother, and slipped under the matching quilt Noa held raised for me.

"Wanna talk 'bout it?" she questioned. In the moon-bright darkness, I could barely make out her features, but I knew my twin's face as well as I knew my own. Even though we weren't identical, growing up with a person — watching them grow and age and *become* someone — you became as familiar with them as if they were a piece of you. I knew she had a mole under her left eye and a scattering of light-colored freckles across her nose and cheeks; knew her eyes, green as moss and always alight with curiosity.

She knew me as well as I knew her, which was apparent in her questioning my readiness to speak about the demons haunting my sleep. I was the older twin, and at some point, had taken on the role as Noa's protector. Refusing to unload my burdens onto Noa had become a cross I willingly bore, even at the expense of my sanity.

Tugging the quilt up higher on her shoulder before brushing her bangs back, I whispered to her, "No, go back to sleep," and she already was.

If I dreamed again that night, I didn't remember it the next morning but terror still lingered in my chest.

Something wicked was brewing.

When I strolled into the kitchen the next morning leaving Noa still sleeping soundly in bed, I was surprised to find our mother bustling around. Mom, notoriously a night owl, did not typically grace us with her presence on weekends until well after midday, so seeing her so close to dawn was startling.

Made even more so because she appeared to be... baking?

The mother I knew barely functioned before two p.m. and never without multiple cups of tea in her system, and judging by the lack of cups by the sink, I knew she had not yet indulged in her obsession for tea.

Narrowing my eyes, I glanced at our lurcher, Lore, for any hint of emergency, but he just gave a doggy smile and thumped his tail softly against the floor where he lay sprawled at Mom's feet.

I crossed my arms as I leaned against the door frame. "Who are you and what have you done with my mother?"

Laughing, Mom looked back at me from over her shoulder, her long, wild curls already escaping from the large clip she had attempted to tame the boisterous mane with. Her eyes, though they were the same agrestal, earthy green as mine and Noa's, Aisling Bishop's were vibrant; sharp with wisdom and a fierce edge that came with the injustices she'd faced in her life. She wore lines gracefully around her mouth, for laughter found her easily and often despite her hardships. Gray lightened her temples, adding sparkling highlights to her hair when the sun caught on the auburn strands.

My mother was a striking woman. Odd, and beautiful; a force to be reckoned with. My father called her a hurricane.

"Ezzie," she called. "Ez, come here. Come help me with these lavender rolls. And please, for the love of spirits, scratch my nose for me." Mom attempted to scrub her nose on her shoulder but couldn't reach. Letting out a plaintive whine, she looked at me with eyes sorrowful enough she could have learned the look from Lore and his begging theatrics.

Sighing histrionically, I walked into the kitchen, swiping my apron from its hook off the wall on the way. Once my apron was secured, bow firmly tied behind my back, I held up my palm for Mom to scrub her nose against. We both laughed at her sigh of relief when the itch was satisfied. After washing my hands, I settled beside Mom. She was in the middle of kneading dough and somehow managed to get flour on multiple surfaces beyond the one she was working on.

Shaking my head fondly, I asked, "All right. Where do you want me to start?"

"Can you make the lavender sugar?" Mom pointed

out the ingredients and I grabbed the food processor before swiping a few sprigs of dried lavender from our wall of drying herbs and flowers. Measuring out the sugar, I poured it into the processor before adding the lavender and hitting the blend button.

Once the lavender sugar was blended, I began on the lemon filling. It was just a matter of melting butter in a small pot with fresh lemon zest. With the bright zing of citrus perfuming the air, I poured the melted butter into a bowl and whisked in cardamon and the floral sugar before mixing the filling together. I passed the bowl to my mom and she spread it over the flat dough evenly before rolling it up lengthwise, cutting even slices, and placing the swirled pieces into a ceramic dish to rise once more.

The morning sun shone in dazzling rays, glinting off the crystals hanging before the window. Mature pothos vines intertwined around most of the kitchen, trellises hanging from the ceiling and atop doorways to the give the sprawling plant places to creep and grow. Numerous white candles were burning on a shelf, the wax trailing on the wood. Everywhere I looked were pieces and parts of the three of us, with shadows of Dad.

Our house felt like its own brand of magic.

Mom brewed up some tea as we chatted, and Noa joined us as we moved out to the back yard to enjoy our warm beverage in the garden. Lore trailed on our heels, claws clicking lightly on the stone patio. I watched as he sniffed around the rose bushes lining the fence, spooking a hiding rabbit into flight. Lore took off in pursuit, his run quick and loping, but the rabbit was already darting for a small hole in the fence. The lurcher had to slam on his breaks or risk crashing headfirst into the solid wood fence — not that it would be the first time.

The sky was a blushing pink, full of yellow and orange clouds surrounding the rising sun. Dew glistened on the grass, glittering brightly in the sunlight like tiny diamonds in an ocean of green. Cradling my warm cup, I inhaled the aroma of the herbal tea as I listened to the happy chatter of morning birds and the soft laughter of Noa and Mom.

I wanted to take these days and press them between the pages of a book. Keep them safe, locked away in my memories forever. These perfect, beautiful summer mornings where nothing bad could go wrong.

When we were all down to the dregs of our tea, Mom sent Noa inside to place the freshly risen lemon-lavender rolls into the oven. Lore's long, sighthound snout was resting comfortably in my lap as I gently stroked his forehead. He had streaks of white in his dark, soot-colored fur where flour had splattered on him.

"Ezra," Mom called, and I turned to her immediately — she rarely called me by my full name. But she wasn't even looking at me; she was gazing, transfixed, into the tea mug clasped tightly between her hands. "Watch out for Noa, okay?"

Brow furrowing, I replied, "Of course, I always do." I chewed on the inside of my cheek in contemplation while I waited for Mom to reply. When it appeared she wasn't going to, I peeked at the kitchen window and seeing Noa at the sink, I inquired in a quiet voice, "Mom, what is going on?"

Seemingly snapped out of the daze she had been in, Mom looked at me.

The look on her face was haunting.

Before I could open my mouth to speak, to question what had caused such fear in her, she wiped the horror from her countenance and put a smile on her face.

"Oh, posh. Don't worry about me," Mom said, waving her hands as if to erase the eerie tension. "Anyway, the real reason I was up and about this morning is because I wanted to give something to you, Ezzie."

Startled, I sat back. My movement upset Lore, for he lost the comfortable pillow of my lap with the sudden movement. He gave a doggy grumble before lumbering off into the grass to collapse in the shade of a tree. Mom was pulling a strand of leather off her head, the small clasp in the back catching on the wild mess of her bun for a moment before gently coming loose, and then she was standing, walking over to me, and placing the leather strand over my head.

At the end of the necklace was a large, raw cut pendant of malachite wrapped lightly in gold wire to secure it to the leather.

"Mom…" I started, but she shushed me before I could finish.

Because I knew this necklace. Dad had given it to her when they first started dating and she *never* took it off.

"It's yours now, Ez. Okay?" Mom crouched down before me, her face beautiful and sad and gentle. Tucking my dark hair behind my ear, she said, "Wear it all the time, my strong girl. Let it help keep the darkness at bay."

She tugged me in close, hugging me tightly. "I love you, Ezra. More than you know. You and Noa mean everything to me. Watch her." Without giving me time to reply, she kissed my forehead and minced into the kitchen, calling Noa's name in a lively, happy tone.

I stared down at the pendant dangling at my chest, and grasped the malachite in my hand. It was still warm from my mother's skin.

The uneasy, restless feeling that had been lingering from the nightmare wrestled to the forefront, swallowing the safe and peaceful presence that had settled over me in the garden from being with my family. I frowned at the pendant, wondering at its purpose and meaning as a gift. Wondering why now, of all times.

Noa and Mom's laughter carried out through the open kitchen window and Noa called my name, beckoning me to come inside to try freshly baked lemon-lavender rolls. Calling for Lore, I headed toward the house, tucking the pendant inside my shirt as I went, thoughts still swirling around my head like a turbulent sea.

I couldn't let go of the thought that Mom was saying goodbye.

About The Author

Salem Sinclair drinks too much coffee, swears like a sailor, doesn't wear matching socks, and survives on slasher films and true crime podcasts. She has a full-time desk job on top of being an author + she's the mom of a pretty rad pre-teen. She also hates talking about herself in these things and never knows what to say.

Made in the USA
Monee, IL
21 December 2021

86601805R00065